FOR MAX, who I just KNOW is going to LOVE books

First published in Great Britain in March 2016 by Bloomsbury Publishing Plc
Published in the United States of America in June 2017
by Bloomsbury Children's Books • www.bloomsbury.com
Bloomsbury is a registered trademark of Bloomsbury Publishing Plc

For information about permission to reproduce selections from this book, write to
Permissions, Bloomsbury Children's Books, 1385 Broadway, New York, New York 10018
Bloomsbury books may be purchased for business or promotional use. For information
on bulk purchases please contact Macmillan Corporate and Premium Sales Department at
specialmarkets@macmillan.com

Library of Congress Cataloging-in-Publication Data
available upon request
ISBN 978-1-68119-323-6 (hardcover)

Art created with multimedia and digital collage
Typeset in Clarendon
Book design by Goldy Broad
Printed in China by C & C Offset Printing Co., Ltd., Shenzhen, Guangdong
10 9 8 7 6 5 4 3 2 1

All papers used by Bloomsbury Publishing, Inc., are natural, recyclable products
made from wood grown in well-managed forests. The manufacturing processes
conform to the environmental regulations of the country of origin.

A PLACE to READ

A Place to READ

Leigh Hodgkinson

BLOOMSBURY

NEW YORK LONDON OXFORD NEW DELHI SYDNEY

The thing is . . .

when I want to read,

what I REALLY

REALLY need

is a place to sit . . .

just for a bit.

Somewhere comfy.

But NOT buzz-buzzy.

And NOT all
growly, itchy,
FUZZY.

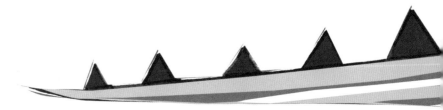

Some place brighter.

WITHOUT these

H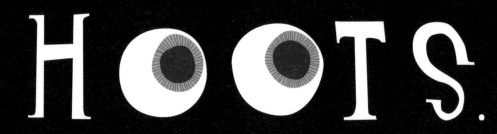OTS.

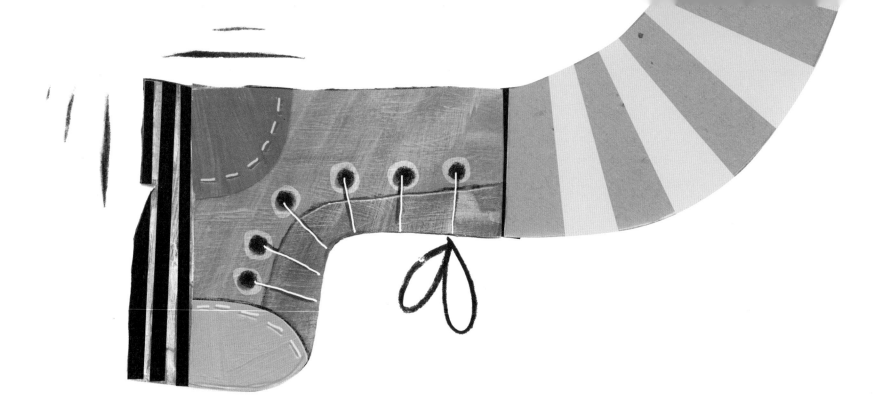

And "NO!" to

GIANT

STOMPING boots.

A place NOT smelly,

StinKY,

grimy.

Somewhere nice. NOT *slippy*, slimy.

(And I don't like SOGGY—sorry, Froggy!)

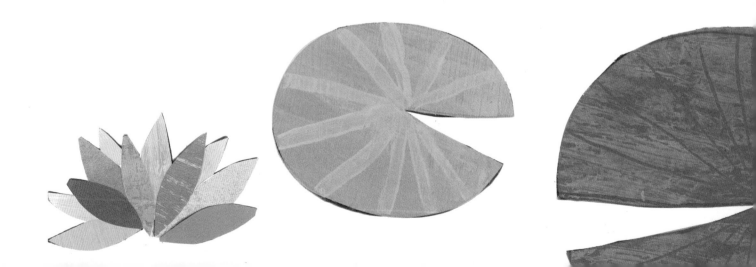

But it can't be far—

SORRY, star!

It's

to be NOT hot, you see.

And NOT too

c o l d...

...or up a TREE.

(This is WAY too high for me!)

Is this so very much to *ask*?

It seems to be a __MIGHTY__ task.

But wait, hang on—

YES

THAT'S IT!

It doesn't matter

where you sit . . .

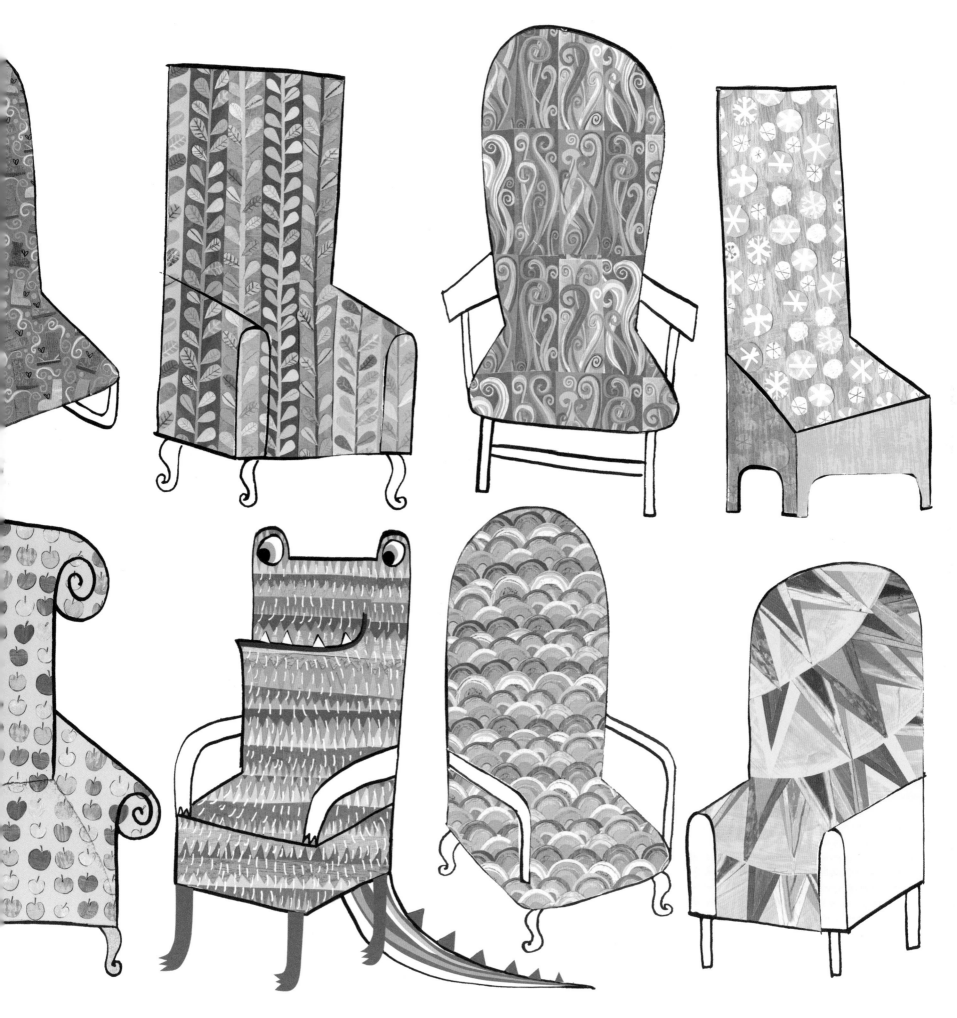

...a book is best **anywhere**...

a book is best when you
SHARE.

All read
happily
EVER AFTER.

And the boy, the cat,
the monster, the fox,
the butterfly, the
mouse, the frog, the
martian, the lion,
the polar bear,
and the bird...